# Tales from Cabin-Knot
## Flight in the Night!

by Bruce Wayne and Jeannette O. Stender
Illustrated by Shonte and Latoya Jones

Stories from real life, about a real place, about real creatures—with illustrations of the creatures that tell the real story. Animals don't really talk, at least not in English.

ISBN 978-1-68570-362-2 (paperback)
ISBN 978-1-68570-363-9 (digital)

Christian Faith Publishing
832 Park Avenue
Meadville, PA 16335
www.christianfaithpublishing.com

Stories from real life, about a real place, about real creatures—with illustrations of the creatures that tell the real story. Animals don't really talk, at least not in English.

For the fifth anniversary of the Party Rock Fire, we offer this in thanksgiving to the glory of God and for the joy of life from the original guardians of the forest and great helpers:

Caleb and Cassian

BJ, Jaylen, Robert, and Rylan

# Foreword

God has given us a marvelous world full of wonder! We only have to look around with our eyes wide open to be able to see it and learn some of its lessons. The stories and adventures included here are based on real events but told from the perspective of the creatures of the forest.

In 2016, a rolling log from a campfire on Party Rock near Lake Lure, North Carolina, started a fire that grew to cover over 7,100 acres in three counties, Rutherford, Hendersonville, and Buncombe. In Buncombe County on Shumont Mountain, over 250 firefighters per day from all across the country and every county in North Carolina fought to protect the lives and homes of residents. Many who helped were flatlanders, totally unfamiliar with fighting fire in mountainous terrains with narrow, curvy roads that resemble cow paths on the edge of a mountain and without road signs. From November 5–21, 2016, thanks to the grace of God and the labors of so many first responders, three things happened:

1. The fire was put out.
2. Not a single human life was lost. The only injuries were sprained ankles and sore muscles.
3. Not a single structure was lost, from the $10 tent to the multi-million-dollar home.

As you read this story, know that it is much more than just a story. May it inspire you to become a guardian of the forest.

# Chapter 1

# Flight in the Night!

Near the crest of Shumont Mountain, nestled in the hard woods and mountain laurels, sits a cozy log cabin. This is not an old run-down cabin and not so new as to smell of paints and stains, but a comfy cabin. The logs are made from big pines and full of knots. So the family who lives there calls it Cabin-Knot.

On one side of Cabin-Knot is a frog pond. The pond is many things to many critters. Bear and deer, bunnies and chipmunks, frogs and hawks, and songbirds of every kind, all come to this pond to drink, eat, splash, wash, and watch.

The pond changes during every season of the year. Some winters, the pond is so frozen that a bear could walk across it. The croaking of the frogs in the spring keeps everyone awake. In the summer, the dragonflies, butterflies, bees, and hummers make about as much noise as the frogs.

And in the autumn, there are no words to describe all the colors of the leaves. When they fall, the forest floor is covered deep, like a beautifully painted carpet.

You can hear the crinkle and crackle of the leaves as Chippy dashes back and forth to his tunnel. Chippy is a dark-brown chipmunk with bold stripes along his sides. He is the busybody of the pond. Running is his favorite thing to do. He races to gather seeds, dashes back to his tunnel to store them, and does this routine over again and over again. He doesn't travel far on his short little legs, but he runs! He is always checking on what's new in the forest from all the animals that pass by.

One late fall afternoon, Chippy was just settling in to his warm bed chamber for the night. Suddenly, the ground shook so hard he thought his tunnel would crash in. He ran to the opening of his tunnel and slowly peeked out. The rumbling of many hooves was getting louder.

"Who's out there?" Chippy called. In the last of the setting sunlight and first beams of moonlight, he caught a glimpse of a family of deer racing up the meadow by the stream. "Wait! Where are you going?"

"Run! Hide! Danger is coming!" shouted Brooster, the lead deer.

Jenny cautioned, "Quick, kids! Don't fall behind! We must stay up with Papa!"

"Please, Momma, can we get a quick drink?" pleaded Tallia.

"Be quick!" Momma Jenny called back. "I can still see where Papa is going! Hurry!"

"The sky is all red!" Tasha yelled. "It's hot and smells awful!"

Tallia licked her lips and said, "It's coming quickly right behind us!"

Chippy looked down the creek and saw a flicker of light. He caught a whiff of something.

"Let's go!" hurried Jenny, and the deer were off in a flash!

Suddenly, Chippy remembered what the smell was. "It's a fire!" He raced back into his tunnel. He ran past his bedroom and headed down the longest escape tunnel.

Out into the night he dashed. He ran and ran. Quick as a flash, he passed over the top of the hill. Then, without any warning, he felt the blast of a cold, wet wind. In the next second, Chippy was completely drenched.

He wiped his eyes, and then he saw it—a big red giant! It roared! It was so loud—louder than the frogs in the pond! He saw tall creatures nearby with two glowing stripes around their legs and arms! Some of them were beating the ground with a strange stick! Others were holding up a long, yellow stick that was shooting rain out of one end.

"That is what soaked me!" Chippy thought.

Suddenly, a loud shrill came from one of the creatures. Quickly, they all climbed on board the big red giant. A roaring noise from the giant grew louder as it moved toward Chippy. He dashed out of the way, just in time, as the giant moved past him and headed toward the pond.

Chippy raced back to his tunnel. He reached the opening and scurried in. That strange smell filled the tunnel. The air was like fire, but it smelled old and wet. He ran all the way to the doorway by the pond and froze in his tracks. He heard the loud noise again, like the one he heard at the top of the hill. He slowly peeked out.

And there it was again!

"It's the big red giant with all the strange creatures moving around it! They have those big yellow sticks with rain shooting out!" he yelled. "They are shooting rain on the fire." All Chippy could see now was a little bit of white smoke slowly floating up from the place where the fire used to be.

"These strange creatures are fighting the fire with water!" Now Chippy realized these creatures were helping him and all his forest friends. They stopped the fire before it ever reached Chippy, the pond, and Cabin-Knot! He watched for a long while as the creatures moved back and forth to make sure all the fire was out.

*What great fighters they are!* thought Chippy. *I'll call them firefighters, and I'll tell everyone what they did!*

He watched and he waited. The first rays of the morning sun were just coming over the mountain. All the firefighters climbed back into the big red giant. Then, more noises that sounded even louder came from the giant as it slowly moved back up the hill.

*I wonder what the firefighters call that big red giant?* he thought.

WHAT WOULD YOU CALL IT?

By now, Chippy was so tired that he couldn't even run. He slowly crawled back into his tunnel, headed to his bed, and fell asleep. He dreamed of how blessed he was that the firefighters stopped the fire from reaching his home, the pond, and Cabin-Knot.

Chippy slept late that next morning. It was almost noon when he woke up. When he looked out his door, he saw Brooster talking with Jenny.

24

"Our old home has changed," explained Brooster. "This morning when I looked down the creek, all of the bushes we used to hide in are gone. The ground is black. There are no berries anywhere for us to eat. I'm afraid we'll have to move to the other side of the mountain."

"Oh, Brooster," said Jenny sadly. "I really don't want to move the kids from our woods, but we must find food!"

"We'll be all right. We still have our family. We'll find another meadow with lots of berries. Let's get started!" said Brooster.

"But, Brooster!" called Chippy. "Will you come back to visit us?" But in an instant, Brooster, Jenny, Tallia, and Tasha had already bounded out of sight. *I hope they will visit soon*, thought Chippy. He was sad that his friends were leaving, but he knew they had to find food where they could. He was happy that the pond, his other friends, and Cabin-Knot were all safe. He remembered the creatures that fought the fire, and he gave God thanks for them. He couldn't wait to tell all his other friends of his all-night adventure, and off he raced.

# About the Illustrators

Shonte Jones is an art novice who enjoys playing with color. She attended the University of Florida, where she received a BFA in studio drawing. She is an aspiring Christian artist who explores the Gospel through acrylic fluid artwork. Shonte works and lives in Charleston, South Carolina, with her son Robert, her sister Latoyya, and her niece Rylan and nephew Jaylen.

Charleston native, Latoyya Jones graduated from Florida State University with a BS in studio art. She is the single mother of two children, Jaylen and Rylan. God has blessed her with a unique artistic style to share with you.

# About the Authors

Jeannette and Bruce Stender have owned their property on Shumont Mountain in rural Buncombe County since 1986. Through the grace of God and over that time, experience has been a phenomenal teacher. They have been married for forty-seven years. There has never been a time when they have not known Jesus as their Lord and Saviour while still needing His forgiveness.

Jeannette was a public school teacher for two years, taught physical education for twenty-two years at the O'Quinn's School in Charleston, South Carolina, ran the Episcopal bookstore at the Cathedral of St. Luke at St. Paul for nine years, founded a daycare at Christ School for taking care of faculty children for seven years, loved and raised two kids, two grand boys, and two step-grandchildren, and taught her husband everything he knows.

Bruce was a marine biologist with SCDNR for thirty years, taught as an adjunct at the College of Charleston and Trident Technical College, served as the coordinator for college ministry for the Diocese of South Carolina for six years, for over twelve years was a teacher, wrestling coach, head of the science department, and head of house for Cunningham House at Christ School, and is now continuing to serve as a captain and EMT with the Broad River Volunteer Fire Department for six years.

Lightning Source UK Ltd.
Milton Keynes UK
UKRC030952190722
406068UK00001B/12